• 11 Cobbler's shop   • 12 Tailor's shop   • 13 Gypsy camp   • 14 Ropemakers   • 15 Tinker   • 16 Weaver's shop   • 17 Village store   • 18 Toy maker's shop   • 19 Potter's shop   • 20 Glazier's workshop

· PHILIPPE FIX ·

Not So Very Long Ago

LIFE IN A SMALL

COUNTRY VILLAGE

DUTTON CHILDREN'S BOOKS   NEW YORK

One hundred or so years ago, your great-great-grandparents were probably alive. They may have lived in America like you do, but it's also possible that they lived in another country. Many of the families in the United States today originally came from Europe, bringing with them traditions and skills from their native lands.

In those days, television did not exist yet. Radios, motion pictures, and automobiles were ideas fresh from the design shop. Few people had seen these inventions; most had only heard rumors about them, especially in the smaller towns. People spent their time very differently from the way we do today. This is a book about what it was like to live then.

$\mathcal{N}$ot so very long ago, peddlers roamed the countryside for months at a stretch. In summer and winter, rain and snow, they went from town to town, selling their wares throughout their usual districts. They also passed messages from family to family along the route, the way postmen now deliver letters. The lucky peddler who was rich enough to own a horse would stop by the blacksmith to check on his horse's shoes before he left. Whether on horse or on foot, the peddler always carried in his pack something for everyone: buttons, baubles, spoons, scissors, ribbons, tools, toys, beads, combs, cloth, linens, gadgets...

Anton is a peddler who has just returned from a month-long trip. His family is very glad to have him home, especially because the village fair will take place in just a few days. The fair is one of the biggest events of the year.

Anton travels on foot. During his journeys, he spends the night at roadside inns. In the evenings, he exchanges stories and barters for goods with other peddlers, while the innkeeper serves a hot meal. When he gets home, his children are eager to see what new books and presents he has bargained from his fellow travelers. This time he brought Laura and John a new almanac. An almanac is a good book for the whole family. It contains jokes, stories, weather forecasts, the dates of important holidays and fairs, and even horoscopes.

While Anton is on the road, his wife, Elizabeth, stays home and keeps house. To earn extra money for the family, she also does odd jobs while Laura and John are at school.

In the village, boys and girls go to different classes and have different teachers. Each morning, Laura and John separate. They line up for inspection with their classmates. If their fingernails or hands are dirty, they are sent home to wash.

Each boy in John's class has a notebook, pens and pencils, a small chalkboard, and a counting abacus for doing sums. The schoolmaster reads stories and poems aloud to the class, and sometimes the children must copy the poems in their notebooks to memorize them for recitation. At the age of twelve, most boys leave school so they can learn the family business from their fathers. Some girls leave school, as well, to help out at home.

After school, Laura and John like to play in the village with their friends. Sometimes they shoot marbles or play with a hoop and stick or give each other rides in a wagon. There are always many people to look at and shops to visit. Tradesmen continually wander up and down the street, advertising their goods and services by singing little songs. "Knife sharp-en-er, knife sharp-en-er . . . Bring your russs-ty blades!"

When an old man and his donkey come by with a calliope, the children stop their games. They run to listen to the music that plays as the entertainer turns the handle of his instrument. When he finishes, they give him a few coins as thanks.

The tailor's shop is one of the children's favorite places to visit. The tailor is teaching Laura how to make a doll's dress. John likes to listen to the tailor's stories and the gossip that he shares as he sews.

Before he could afford his own shop, the tailor traveled the countryside like a peddler, staying with one rich family after another for two or three days while he made them new clothes. Any family with a wedding planned was the best find of all. A bride's trousseau often took several weeks to sew. During his travels, the tailor collected many entertaining anecdotes.

The tailor buys his cloth from the village weaver. The weaver's shop is built on a clay floor, slightly below ground, so the air is dusky, cool, and humid. Moisture is important for making fine, strong thread that will not break easily.

The weaver sits on a stool as his feet drive the pedals of the loom. With his hands, he throws the shuttle back and forth. Then he lets the heavy shaft fall, pushing the new threads tightly into the piece of fabric. Meanwhile, his wife works at the spinning wheel, spinning the thread out of cotton flax and spooling it onto the shuttles that feed the loom.

Not far from the weaver's shop is the village glassblower, or glazier. The glazier makes bottles, mirrors, vials, and jars for all the shops and homes in the area. John and Laura love to watch him work.

The glazier uses a great deal of wood in his shop for the fires he builds. He melts the glass over the fire. A fire must be very, very hot to melt glass. When it does melt, the glazier uses a long, hollow pipe to pull a glob of glass paste out of the oven. Quickly the apprentice twirls the stem back and forth between his hands, blowing through the pipe, while the glazier shapes the glass with a wooden tool.

When the glass balloon is just the right size for the object he is making, the glazier makes the neck of the object with pliers and then snips off the end with shears, to make the opening. After he has finished an object, he must reheat and cool it once more to strengthen it or else the glass will shatter at the lightest touch.

The village potter and his wife work together in their shop. The potter kicks his wheel into motion with one foot, pumping it to make it spin. Then he throws a lump of clay onto the wheel. With his hands, he rounds out the clay, hollows it in the center, then pulls it up to make it as tall as he likes. When he is satisfied, he stops the wheel and runs a wire underneath the bottom of the piece to remove it. If it is a jug, he then fashions a spout and some handles from another piece of clay and attaches them by hand.

When the jug dries, the potter's wife paints it with a colorful glaze, using a goose quill for a paintbrush. Then the jug is fired in the kiln — a very hot oven that sets the glaze and makes the jug hard and sturdy. The kiln uses so much wood for heating that the potter fires it only once a month.

Occasionally, Laura and John go into the forest beyond the village gate to hunt for mushrooms. Their mother cooks the mushrooms with meat and soup. But first the children always take their baskets to the local apothecary and show him what they have picked. He knows all about plants and can tell them which kinds of mushrooms are poisonous and which are safe to eat.

Everything in the apothecary's shop is arranged with great care. Bottles of medicines are labeled neatly in Latin. The walls are lined with containers of herbs, salves, and ointments. When anyone gets sick, the apothecary is glad to give advice on the best medicine.

If the children have an extra penny or two, they run to the village store for some candy, marbles, colored pencils, or string for their kites.

The storekeeper knows her way perfectly through the jumble of merchandise. She can always find just what the customer needs: a shoelace, a feather duster, a blue button... Top to bottom, the store is packed with goods. Ropes and sausages hang from the rafters. Barrels and baskets cover the floor, filled with tins of cocoa, bars of soap, bottles of syrup, pots of mustard and molasses, and vegetables galore! Large burlap sacks filled with coffee beans make everything smell delicious. The women of the village love to gather in the store for a chat, to break up the day.

Wooden clogs are practical shoes for country life. The clogmaker has made shoes for Anton's family ever since Anton himself was a little boy. The clogmaker's father and grandfather made clogs, too. Their family has been in the same business for over a hundred years. This clogmaker knows just which trees to cut for the toughest, sturdiest wood. He knows the best time to cut by watching the moon and the weather. He also knows how to carve shoes from blocks of wood with an ax and a plane. When he is finished, his two sons work on each shoe with a rasp until it is smooth and comfortable. The older son then paints and decorates the clogs to match the customer's specifications.

Almost everyone who works outdoors in the village wears wooden clogs. Leather shoes wear out too quickly when they are constantly exposed to the rain, dirt, and snow. Wooden shoes hardly ever wear out. In the wintertime, clogs can be stuffed with straw to keep the feet extra warm. But for special occasions, like feasts and church celebrations, leather shoes are worn.

The cobbler runs the town's shoe repair. He also makes new leather shoes to order, tracing the shape of a customer's foot on a piece of paper for a pattern. Most people can afford to have only one pair of leather shoes, so the cobbler tries to make his footwear as sturdy as possible. Today the bird catcher has come by—his boot has a hole in the bottom from all the walking he has done, strolling up and down the streets of the town while he sells his songbirds.

This village craftsman runs a lathe for making wooden objects.
Like the potter, he works his machinery with his foot. As the spindle
turns, he carefully carves and shapes the revolving blocks of wood.
He makes bowls and eggcups, spinning wheels and rolling pins,
saltshakers and hammers, spoons and mallets, even wooden toys and
bowling pins.

Today his wife is gathering some goods into a basket that they
can carry to sell at the fair. She is in charge of pricing all the goods.

From time to time, John helps them gather wood. In return, the
woodworker will make him a top to spin.

Sometimes the children cannot play because they have to run errands for their mother. Today Laura must bring a pot with a hole in it to the tinker. A tinker is a metalsmith. He can fix anything made out of metal—from pots, pans, and basins to umbrella ribs.

Like peddlers, tinkers travel from town to town. They need only a few tools: pliers, files, a hammer, and a cauldron. To fix a pot with a hole in it, the tinker first cleans the broken part with acid. Meanwhile, he melts a scrap of tin in the cauldron over a hot fire. When the tin becomes liquid, he dunks the broken pot in it. The molten metal fills the hole, and the tinker pounds it into shape with his hammer while holding the pot with his pliers. Then he dips the pot in cold water to cool it. After it is polished and shined, it looks like new.

On very special days, there is a gypsy show in the village square, with dancers, music, magic tricks, and maybe a dancing bear or goat— sometimes even a monkey. All the children in town gather to watch. Laura and John usually give pennies to the performers when the show is over.

Gypsy caravans travel from town to town, putting on shows. Laura and John enjoy the performance, but watching the bears makes them sad. They learned from their father that the gypsy trainers teach the bears to dance by making them step on a burning hot plate that has been roasted in the fire. The bears seem to prance up and down to the music.

When the gypsies are not performing, they do various odd jobs. Many of them are excellent basket weavers. The women also tell fortunes. Gypsies have been wandering through Europe for over five hundred years.

To earn extra money, Elizabeth does a little work for the toy maker and his wife. Laura and John often have to run by the toy shop to pick up or drop off a project for their mother. The shop is another one of their favorite places to go. Elizabeth assembles and paints little penny toys made of tin, wood, or cardboard. Sometimes she sews doll clothes.

The toy maker's great joy is inventing new toys. Today he has just completed a flying machine. He explains to John how a propeller sets the ship in motion.

Laura likes to look at the new doll that the toy maker's wife is dressing. The seamstress makes the doll clothes to match the catalog pictures from Paris. This doll is dressed in the latest fashion.

Before Elizabeth got a job at the toy maker's, she earned money by doing laundry for several families in the neighborhood. Each family hand-washed its shirts and underclothes every week. But two or three times a year, a big laundry of bed linens, tablecloths, and towels had to be done. It took Elizabeth three days to do each big wash.

First, Elizabeth would sort the linens and soak them for a whole day. Then she would line the bottom of the heavy wooden washing vat with straw and add the wet laundry. The water would soak into the straw as it drained off the linens. She would pack all the laundry into the vat, putting bay leaves and tiger-lily roots between each layer to make the linens smell good when they were clean. When the vat was full, she would tuck a cloth over the laundry, cover it with wood ash from the fire, and pour kettles and kettles of boiling water into the vat. The ash in the water acted like a strong soap to clean the clothes. This process was repeated for eight to ten hours. Then the linens were finally taken out, scrubbed again with regular soap, rinsed, dried, ironed, and put away.

Finally the big day has arrived: the village fair! The whole family wakes up early and gets ready to go. Laura and John are so excited they can hardly wait.

The fair takes place just outside of town. Not only villagers but country folk from all around attend. The children's grandparents are coming from their farm in the country, and they plan to take Laura and John back with them to visit for a few days.

At the fair, the noise and bustle is tremendous. Above it all, the auctioneer can be heard. He runs the livestock trading block. First he puts a pig, cow, goat, horse, or bull on the trading block and calls out a sum. Interested buyers in the crowd bargain with him, trying to make him lower his prices. At last, the trader accepts the highest bid, and the two men slap their palms together, high in the air, to close the deal.

Besides the merchants and the tradespeople, there are storytellers and performers at the fair—even a wagon with a magician and an oompah band! There's also a tooth puller who pulls bad teeth for a quarter.

The next day, Laura and John wake up even earlier than the day before, glad to be in the country. Their uncle Leonard is going to take them to his friend, the miller, to show them how flour is made.

Leonard is a shepherd; he pastures his flocks on his parents' land. During warm weather, he lives in a very small hut on wheels—it's so small that he has to crawl in and out on his hands and knees. The wheels allow him to move his home from place to place, following the sheep to good pastures. Leonard has a knack with animals, and his sheepdog helps him keep track of strays by obeying his calls, whistles, and finger snaps.

When Leonard and the children reach the mill, the miller is standing on top of the steps, watching the clouds move across the sky. It's important for him to know when the wind changes direction. If it does, he must change the direction that the wheels inside the mill are turning, to match.

When the wind turns the weather vanes on top of the building, the wooden axle that runs down through the roof turns the top millstone inside. The bottom millstone never moves. The kernels of raw wheat are pressed and ground between the two stones. The wheat powder runs through the grooves in the bottom stone and down into a funnel. The flour is then separated from the larger pieces of chaff by a sieve, and the two portions run out into separate sacks. A little bell rings when all the wheat has been ground so that the millstones will not spark together and start a fire.

One of Laura's favorite games is jumping rope. John and his grandmother are helping his grandfather make a nice long rope for her.

First, her grandfather has to cut the hemp, a tough plant whose fibers make strong cord. Then he must prepare it. He beats away the bark of the hemp and combs the leftover fibers, separating them into fine strands. Then he ties the hemp around his waist and places a bundle on the spinning hook. John turns the handle as Grandfather steps backward, letting the fibers play through his hands while he deftly twists and ties them together. John must turn the handle very smoothly or the rope will be uneven.

Today the mattress maker is coming to visit the farm. Grandmother is giving Anton and Elizabeth a new mattress as a present, and she needs one of her old mattresses fixed as well.

The mattress maker makes new mattresses on the spot or refurbishes old ones that have lost their springiness. She packs up all her tools and brings them with her. To improve the old mattress, she pulls out all the wool-thread stuffing. It has to be aired, plucked, and combed to regain its freshness and shape. Her helper straddles the carding machine and feeds the wool through it. Meanwhile, Anton picks out a fabric for the new mattress ticking. Leonard has brought a bag of fresh wool from his sheep to be carded and stuffed into the ticking.

On the farm, almost everything is handmade. Very few items are bought at the store, and nothing useful is ever thrown away. Even rags are saved and sold to the ragpicker, who comes by with his dog cart every few months to haggle over a piece of moth-eaten fur or a worn-out wool scarf. Grandmother loves to bargain with him. When he leaves, his cart is so heavy that the dogs can barely pull it behind them.

After supper, the whole family stays together in front of the warm oven, next to the kitchen. Grandfather carves for relaxation and enjoyment. Tonight he is finishing a new birdhouse. John is helping him fit the pieces together.

Grandmother knits near the table, while Laura chats and reads aloud. Every once in a while, Grandmother interrupts with a story of her own—sometimes about her childhood, sometimes about the gypsies. When Laura was born, Grandmother said, a gypsy came by and tied a white thread around a willow branch in the yard. That meant a little girl had arrived—a red thread would have meant a boy.

While the children were away at their grandparents', Elizabeth barely left the kitchen back at home. She has been baking cakes, pies, and cookies for St. John's Day, the biggest feast of the year. St. John is the guardian saint of the village, and little John was named after him.

By the time Laura, John, and their grandparents arrive in town, people from all over the countryside already have begun to gather in front of the chapel. Soon the chapel bells ring, announcing the beginning of the mass. The chapel is so full that latecomers must crowd on the steps outside. The air is filled with the sweet smell of incense, and the choir begins to sing.

After mass, people approach the altar to give their offerings, lighting a candle for St. John and thanking him or asking his help. Mothers try to banish evil by leaving a shirt or hat of one of their children next to the altar. Many of the sick drink from the holy spring that bubbles behind the chapel, hoping to heal themselves with its waters.

The street singer tells stories both dramatic and comic, while the audience follows the adventure in the painted scenes on the screen next to the performer. An old man with a black robe and a long beard wanders through the crowd, telling children stories about the saints.

Grandmother has brought several food baskets of her own. She and Elizabeth spread out a picnic for the family. Just before lunch, John wins a contest—he is the first to successfully climb the greased holiday pole! He gives his mother the coupon he has won for two pounds of sugar.

In the evening, a bonfire is lit, and all the children dance around it, hand in hand. When the fire burns down, the most daring try to leap over it—this brings them luck for the new year. When Laura and John rejoin their parents, they find that Anton has good news. A fellow peddler has decided to open up a store and is ready to sell his cart and horse for a very fair price! Anton will be able to carry and sell more goods, and his trips will be shorter.

It will be a new and even better life for the family!

Library of Congress Cataloging-in-Publication Data

Fix, Philippe.
[Kaum hundert Jahre ist es her. English]
Not so very long ago: Life in a small country village / by Philippe Fix.
—1st American ed.
p.   cm.
Translation of: Kaum hundert Jahre ist es her.
Summary: Describes daily life as it would have been lived by the reader's
great-great-grandparents, either in the United States or Europe.
ISBN 0-525-44594-3
1. United States—Social life and customs—1865–1918—Juvenile
literature.   2. Europe—Social life and customs—19th century—
Juvenile literature.   [1. United States—Social life and
customs—1865–1918.   2. Europe—Social life and customs—19th
century.]   I. Title.
E168.F5813   1994
973.8—dc20   93-8428 CIP AC

First published in the United States 1994 by Dutton Children's Books,
a division of Penguin Books USA Inc.
375 Hudson Street, New York, New York 10014

Originally published in Germany 1987 by Ravensburger Buchverlag Otto Maier GmbH
Original German title: *Kaum hundert Jahre ist es her*

Typography by Barbara Powderly

Printed in Hong Kong   First American Edition
10 9 8 7 6 5 4 3 2 1

THE COUNTRY

- 1 Grandfather and Grandmother's house
- 2 Uncle Leonard's winter house
- 3 Mattress maker's house
- 4 Grandfather's field
- 5 Grandmother's beehives
- 6 Well
- 7 Grocery store
- 8 Washhouse
- 9 Clogmaker's workshop
- 10 Woodworker's hut